TREETURE CREATURES
AND
FLOWERBUDS

I would like to dedicate this book to my wonderful big sisters.
Teresa Crowley and Eileen Stapleton, you have shared so much
throughout my life and I feel blessed to be able to call you
my friends and my family.
Thank you, I love you both very much.

Published in the United Kingdom by:

Blue Falcon Publishing
The Mill, Pury Hill Business Park,
Alderton Road, Towcester
Northamptonshire NN12 7LS
Email: books@bluefalconpublishing.co.uk
Web: www.bluefalconpublishing.co.uk

A CIP record of this book is available from the British Library.

First printed September 2021
ISBN 97819127652348

Beech the
Beech Leaf

Marian Hawkins

From its hefty canopy, the beech leaf flutters down,

Landing beside Dandelion who eyes her with a frown.

"I'm on a special journey," declares a smiling Beech,

As a fluffy pappus floats nearby, just out of reach.

Suddenly, a football lands and Beech sticks to its leather.

Beech is launched across the park, floating like a feather.

She peels herself away, relieved to be on solid ground,

Then smiles and greets Horse Chestnut, a new friend that

she has found.

"Howdy, Horse Chestnut, do you think you're from my tree?
I was launched here on a football; perhaps you can help me?"
Horse Chestnut says,
"Neigh, sorry, but my oval lobes are long,
Shaped just like a hand, with toothed edges all along.
My tree makes shiny conkers, safe in prickly green cases.
Children pick them up and hang the best ones from shoelaces.
The conkers left upon the ground become food for the deer.
It's said, put conkers in your house
and spiders will keep clear."
Beech smiles, "Well, this has been nice,
but you're not from my tree."
"I'm not; it's the horse chestnut tree
that must belong to me."

A Labrador comes over, keenly sniffing all around.
Beech gets stuck upon his paw and stamped into the ground.
Looking up, she sees a pretty snowdrop, pearly white.
"Hi, Snowdrop, I hope I haven't given you a fright.
I am having fun, but hope to find my tree today.
Snowdrop giggles, "Good luck, Beech; I'll let you on your way."

When Beech sees Sycamore, she asks him,
"Are you from my tree?
I came here squished on a dog's paw;
perhaps you can help me?"
Sycamore grins, "No, my lobes are pointed at the top.
My fruits spin round just like
a helicopter's blades when dropped.
Wooden spoons and bowls are carved out of my wood.
It is very strong, so for utensils it is good.
Sycamores can live long lives and they grow very tall.
My flowers offer nectar and small birds eat seeds that fall.
Beech nods, "Nice to meet you,
but you are not from my tree."
"That's right," her friend agrees.
"The sycamore belongs to me."

A pink kite floats down with a squelch and
Beech sticks to its frame.
With a gust, the kite lifts off — what a super game!
Not airborne for long, the kite lands —
Splat! — in a new place,
Beside Forget-me-not, who's tiny,
blue, and full of grace.
Forget-me-not says, "Hello Beech,
I hear you've lost your way."
"Yes, that's right," smiles Beech.
"I'm having quite a thrilling day!"

As Beech moves on, she meets with Spruce:
"Hi! Are you from my tree?
I flew in on a pretty kite, perhaps you can help me?"
"My leaf has short, stiff needles that smell so very sweet.
My tree produces woody cones that squirrels like to eat.
My shape is tall and pointed, like a giant green triangle.
At Christmas, from my branches shiny,
sparkly baubles dangle.
Prince Albert famously began this decorating trend.
It is a very festive tree indeed, my dear friend."
Beech says, "It's been a pleasure,
but you are not from my tree."
"Ho, ho, no!" laughs Spruce.
"It's the spruce tree that belongs to me."

"After sticking to a ball, by a black Lab I was found.
I flew up on a kite, after being squashed into the ground.
The wind blew me far, far away from where I'm meant to be.
Will I ever get back home to my majestic, tall beech tree?"
Beech closes her eyes and she whooshes into the air,
Then floats down wondering, "Am I home now, am I there?
Yippee! Home at last." Beech sees all of her leafy friends.
"It's my tree! Beech is the name, so here my journey ends.
My wonderful beech tree is often thought of as a queen.
Under my canopy, what grows beneath is rarely seen.
My leaves are oval, with a pointed tip and a wavy edge.
Sometimes beech is used in gardens in place of a hedge.
My tree produces nuts that grow in small, spiky green cases;
They are fed to pigs, who scoff them, putting smiles
on their faces!
Moth caterpillars eat my leaves before they all take flight.
In ancient times, beech oil was used for keeping lamps alight."
As autumn comes, Beech turns shades of yellow and red,
Waiting for the spring, with friends Beech lays her head.
When winter's passed, new growth peeks through the earth,
Then we can enjoy the beauty of springtime's new birth.
"Adventure over," Beech smiles, "and it's really been such fun!
I've met great buds, leaves and trees, each a special one."
Now you can explore, and see which ones you can find.
Look after our buds and trees, and make sure to be kind!"

The Importance of Trees

As well as visual benefits of being around trees, like reducing stress and blood pressure, they have many benefits within the world of medicine, too.

- Aspirin, which is used for pain relief and anti-clotting, is sourced from the willow bark.
- The tannin from oak bark is used as a disinfectant.
- Alder bark contains salicin, which is used as an anti-inflammation treatment.
- Seeds from the ash tree are used to treat irritation and itchy conditions.
- The sap from maple trees has been known to lower blood pressure and in some case prevent ulcers.
- Native Americans used beech leaves as a treatment for tuberculosis.
- The cacao tree produces cacao beans, best known for making chocolate (yum yum). These beans contain theobromine, which also helps in the treatment of asthma.

There are many reasons trees are important.
Here are just a few!

Trees **clean** the air.   They provide **shelter** for wildlife.

They enhance areas with their **beauty**.

They **stabilise** soil.   They offer **shade** and wind breaks.

They help with **flood** control. They help with **noise** reduction.

They are great **fun** to climb, too.   They **produce** oxygen.

They supply us with wonderful **food**.

In the UK only 13% of our land is covered by forests.
In comparison to other European countries this is low.

Apart from being pretty, tree products are used in so many ways in medicine.

Crossword

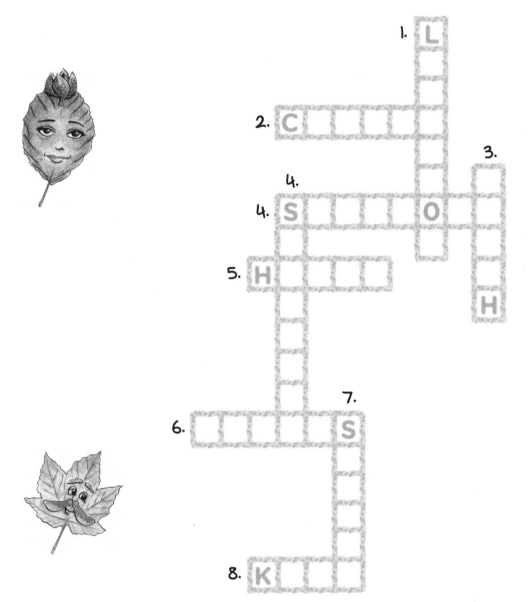

Across

2. Found in a spiky case
4. My fruits spin like helicopter blades
5. A type of chestnut – this leaf may say neigh
6. A fluffy clock of a dandelion
8. Pink and colourful flying in the sky

Down

1. Beech was squashed on his paw
3. Queen of trees
4. White wild flower
7. Christmas tree

Answers
Across
2. Conker
4. Sycamore
5. Horse
6. Pappus
8. Kite

Down
1. Labrador
3. Beech
4. Snowdrop
7. Spruce

Tree truths

Beech

Beech is considered the queen of trees.
Produces beech nuts enclosed in beech masts.
A dense canopy prevents most plants from
growing underneath.
Beech leaves are believed to have medicinal benefits.

Sycamore

The sycamore leaf is described as
palmate. (palm-like)
Its v-shaped winged fruits are also
known as samaras.
They have a strong wood and
are tolerant of pollution.
Leaf stalks on young trees are red.

Spruce

Spruce is evergreen, meaning it does not lose its
needles.
They are tall and triangular.
Most known for use as Christmas trees.
They can live to be 1000 years old.

Horse Chestnut

Produces the conker protected in green spiky cases.
Conkers have been used in medicine for horses.
Myth: conkers keep spiders away.
Its leaves have 5-7 leaflets.

Weird and Wonderful Trees of the World

The Rainbow Eucalyptus Tree

This stunning tree is native to Southeast Asia Islands, such as Indonesia, Philippines and New Guinea.

The rainbow eucalyptus is a perennial tree, meaning it flowers every year. It is fast growing and grows to heights of more than 240 feet/75 metres.

It is also known as the rainbow gum or the midanao gum.

The beautifully coloured trunk is created by the strips of bark peeling off at different times. What lies beneath is green, but the longer it is exposed, the more the change in colour occurs. The effect is a beautiful multicoloured piece of art. Brown, green, maroon, blue, orange and purple are a magnificent display.

These trees are often planted to decorate landscaped gardens or leisure facilities. This provides stunning views.

The rainbow eucalyptus is a good source of pulpwood, which is used to make paper. Its hardwood is also used for furniture, too. They are best suited to warm climates and full sun, although they need moist soil conditions. The rainbow eucalyptus is a thirsty tree it soaks up moisture from swampy areas. This is beneficial in combating malaria, as it absorbs the liquid where the disease is known to breed.

The rainbow eucalyptus is a constantly changing piece of artwork as no pattern is repeated throughout the process of bark shedding.

Parts Of A Tree

Trees get all their energy to survive through their leaves.
Photosynthesis is the process, I do believe!
By converting water, carbon dioxide and sunlight,
It produces glucose, which keeps trees healthy and upright.
The green pigment called chlorophyll absorbs the sun's rays.
That is why mostly green features in our tree displays.

Branches, twigs and leaves, held up by the trunk, fill the crown.
The bark protects the wood; it's often ridged and greyish brown.
All of these parts help transport goodness around the tree.
Nature supplies these nutrients, all of which are free!

Roots are the part of the tree that grows underneath the ground.
They absorb nourishment and water from the soil around.
The roots keep the tree stable, giving it strength to stand tall.
The central root, the taproot, that is the largest of all.

There are many types of trees, to plant lots more is the aim,
Nature supports our trees; to lose them would be such a shame.
So let's do our bit, plant and look after our lovely trees.
For all our treeture creatures and flowerbuds be kind, please.

Some help with sounds...

photosynthesis sounds like   foh - toh -sin -thoh - sis
Chlorophyll sounds like   klorr - uh - fil

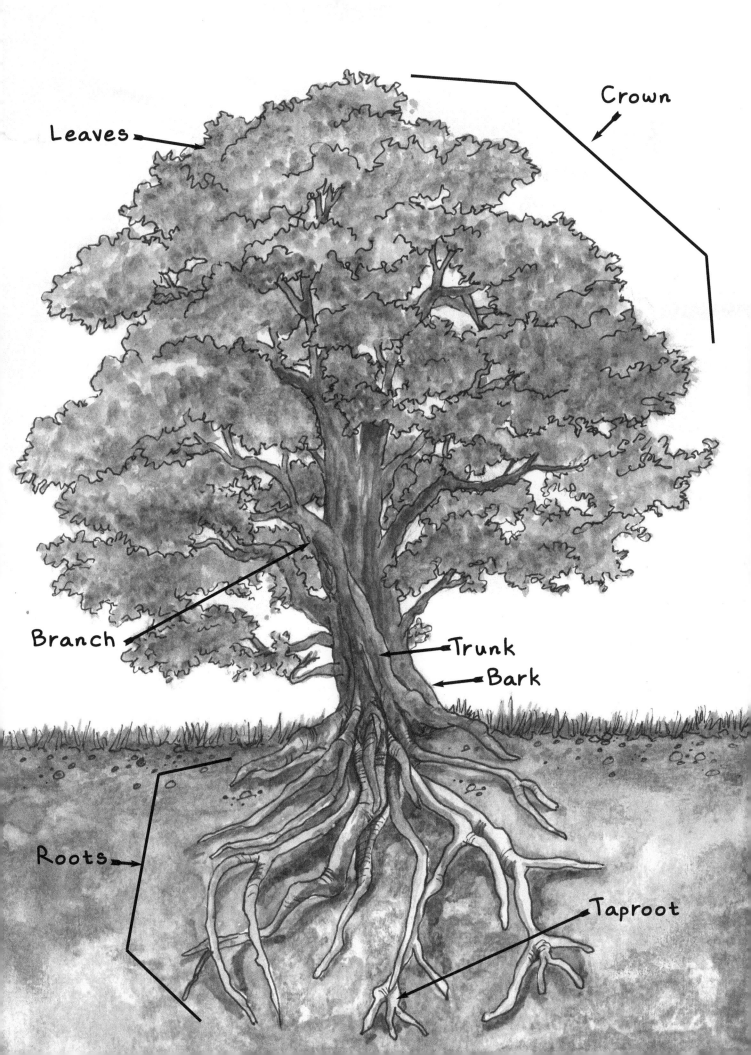

Crown

Leaves

Branch

Trunk

Bark

Roots

Taproot

Treeture Creatures and Flowerbuds
Book 1 – Oaky the Oak Leaf

In this story, we follow Oaky the Oak Leaf on his exciting adventure as he tries to make his way back home and meets some unfamiliar characters on the way!

Available to buy from Amazon, Waterstones and Foyles.

Treeture Creatures and Flowerbuds
Book 2 – Willow the Willow Leaf

It's Willow's turn for an adventure this time, as the little leaf finds himself washed downstream and makes many new friends as he tries to find his way back to where he belongs.

Available to buy from Amazon, Waterstones and Foyles.

Also Available
The Tree Trail Swatch Booklets

Heading out to the park?
Take Oaky and his friends with you on your adventure!
Pop the Tree Trail booklet in your pocket and see how many trees and leaves you can spot on your day out! The booklet will help you identify which leaf is from which tree.
Take pictures and share what you find on your day out with us on Instagram @treeture_creatures_flowerbuds.

ISBN - 9781912765-40-9

Also Available
The Flower Trail Swatch Booklets

Let's go outside!
Take Bluebell and her friends with you on your adventure!
Pop the Flower Trail booklet in your pocket and see how
many wild flowers you can spot on your day out! The booklet
will help you identify wild flowers while you learn interesting
facts. Take pictures and share what you find on your day
out with us on Instagram @treeture_creatures_flowerbuds.
ISBN – 9781912765-41-6

Lightning Source UK Ltd.
Milton Keynes UK
UKHW050308151021
392212UK00002B/83